Samuel French Acting Edition

Admissions

by Joshua Harmon

SAMUELFRENCH.COM   SAMUELFRENCH.CO.UK

Copyright © 2019 by Joshua Harmon
All Rights Reserved

ADMISSIONS is fully protected under the copyright laws of the United States of America, the British Commonwealth, including Canada, and all other countries of the Copyright Union. All rights, including professional and amateur stage productions, recitation, lecturing, public reading, motion picture, radio broadcasting, television and the rights of translation into foreign languages are strictly reserved.

ISBN 978-0-573-70748-3

www.SamuelFrench.com
www.SamuelFrench.co.uk

FOR PRODUCTION ENQUIRIES

UNITED STATES AND CANADA
Info@SamuelFrench.com
1-866-598-8449

UNITED KINGDOM AND EUROPE
Plays@SamuelFrench.co.uk
020-7255-4302

Each title is subject to availability from Samuel French, depending upon country of performance. Please be aware that *ADMISSIONS* may not be licensed by Samuel French in your territory. Professional and amateur producers should contact the nearest Samuel French office or licensing partner to verify availability.

CAUTION: Professional and amateur producers are hereby warned that *ADMISSIONS* is subject to a licensing fee. Publication of this play(s) does not imply availability for performance. Both amateurs and professionals considering a production are strongly advised to apply to Samuel French before starting rehearsals, advertising, or booking a theatre. A licensing fee must be paid whether the title(s) is presented for charity or gain and whether or not admission is charged. Professional/Stock licensing fees are quoted upon application to Samuel French.

No one shall make any changes in this title(s) for the purpose of production. No part of this book may be reproduced, stored in a retrieval system, or transmitted in any form, by any means, now known or yet to be invented, including mechanical, electronic, photocopying, recording, videotaping, or otherwise, without the prior written permission of the publisher. No one shall upload this title(s), or part of this title(s), to any social media websites.

For all enquiries regarding motion picture, television, and other media rights, please contact Samuel French.

MUSIC USE NOTE

Licensees are solely responsible for obtaining formal written permission from copyright owners to use copyrighted music in the performance of this play and are strongly cautioned to do so. If no such permission is obtained by the licensee, then the licensee must use only original music that the licensee owns and controls. Licensees are solely responsible and liable for all music clearances and shall indemnify the copyright owners of the play(s) and their licensing agent, Samuel French, against any costs, expenses, losses and liabilities arising from the use of music by licensees. Please contact the appropriate music licensing authority in your territory for the rights to any incidental music.

IMPORTANT BILLING AND CREDIT REQUIREMENTS

If you have obtained performance rights to this title, please refer to your licensing agreement for important billing and credit requirements.

Originally Produced by Lincoln Center Theater
New York City, 2018

ADMISSIONS was originally produced by Lincoln Center Theater in New York City and premiered on February 15, 2018. The performance was directed by Daniel Aukin, with sets by Riccardo Hernandez, costumes by Toni-Leslie James, lighting by Mark Barton, and sound by Ryan Rumery. The stage manager was Kyle Gates. The cast was as follows:

SHERRI ROSEN-MASON .... Jessica Hecht

BILL MASON .... Andrew Garman

CHARLIE LUTHER MASON............................ Ben Edelman

GINNIE PETERS...................................... Sally Murphy

ROBERTA .... Ann McDonough

CHARACTERS

SHERRI ROSEN-MASON – Early fifties, very liberal secular Jewish woman. Head of Admissions for Hillcrest.

BILL MASON – Early fifties, very liberal WASP, Sherri's husband. Head of the School at Hillcrest.

CHARLIE LUTHER MASON – Seventeen, Bill and Sherri's son, a senior at Hillcrest.

GINNIE PETERS – Fifties, very liberal WASP, stay-at-home mom; her son is Charlie's best friend.

ROBERTA – Early seventies, white, works in development at Hillcrest.

SETTING

The play takes place at Hillcrest, a second-tier, on-the-cusp-of-being-a-first-tier prep/boarding school in rural New Hampshire.

TIME

It begins just before Christmas and ends shortly after Easter, during the 2015-2016 academic year.

This play must be performed without an intermission.

PART ONE: DECEMBER

(Early afternoon. New England winter.
SHERRI, *in her office. A knock at the door.)*

SHERRI. Come in.

*(***ROBERTA*** enters.)*

ROBERTA. Sherri?

SHERRI. Hi Roberta. Come in.

ROBERTA. You wanted to see me?

SHERRI. Come in.

ROBERTA. Because I got a message that you wanted to see me.

SHERRI. Yes, come in!

ROBERTA. Oh, ok.

(She comes in but doesn't close the door.
SHERRI *gets up and closes the door.)*

Can you believe it's almost Christmas break?

SHERRI. I can.

ROBERTA. Guess how many people I have coming for Christmas this year.

SHERRI. How many?

ROBERTA. Guess!

(Quick beat.)

SHERRI. A hundred.

ROBERTA. A hundred! Don't be – twenty-two. Twenty-two Homo sapiens in my house. What's a person to do?

SHERRI. That's a lot of... Homo sapiens.

ROBERTA. It sure is. But if I don't do something about my *mouse* problem –

SHERRI. Oh, I don't –

ROBERTA. I found one little guy – well its corpse anyway – rotting under my sofa.

SHERRI. I don't –

ROBERTA. It smelled like –

SHERRI. Roberta!

I don't have ti– I don't want to hear about the disgusting – about disgusting things. Please?

ROBERTA. I was just telling you about my mouse –

SHERRI. I know. I appreciate the… sharing. But. Let's get to it, ok?

ROBERTA. Oh. Ok.

(Quick beat.)

Is there a problem?

(Beat.)

SHERRI. Yes, Roberta. There's a problem.

ROBERTA. Oh?

SHERRI. Mac sent me the, the, uh, oh for godssake what-do-you-call-it, the draft, the publication draft for the admissions catalogue for next year.

ROBERTA. Oh good, that's all done, and on time, too.

SHERRI. Well, no it's –

ROBERTA. That's been done for two weeks. I believe we sent it to the printer.

SHERRI. No I asked Mac to send me the draft before it went to the printer but I've been a little behind and I didn't get a chance to look at it until today, but…

ROBERTA. That's been done for weeks.

SHERRI. No, it's not done.

ROBERTA. I finished that –

SHERRI. This is not the first time, Roberta, that we have had this conversation, and I don't know why this is so diff–

ROBERTA. What conversation?

SHERRI. Let me finish.

ROBERTA. But I don't –

SHERRI. Let me finish.

I don't know why this is so difficult... *(Unspoken: for you.)* but I'm going to spell it out, *again*, and ask that you really really focus and listen to what I'm saying, ok?

When I first got to Hillcrest, the student body was ninety-four percent white. Six percent students of color. Think about that: For every student of color, there were nineteen white kids. Nineteen to one. Now I have worked like a dog the last fifteen years so that our school looks a little bit more like the country in which it is situated, and today, we're eighteen percent students of color. Which is still an embarrassingly low number, but it's three hundred percent better than where we were just fifteen years ago.

Now, a lot of our applicants can afford to come and look at Hillcrest themselves. Which is great. But not everyone can, and – and not always, certainly not always – but sometimes, those students who cannot afford to visit, are students of color. And the process, the journey of even just applying here is a tremendous one. Tremendous. And despite the high-tech world we are living in, a very important part of their process is they see our catalogue and they bring it home to their parents, or their parents bring it home to their children, and this is their first introduction to Hillcrest. It begins with the Admissions Catalogue. It begins here.

But. If they open up that catalogue, and they don't see anyone who looks like them, that will be the end of their journey. They will not apply. And why should they? Who would want to be the only Black or Hispanic student in some far-away boarding school in New Hampshire, where they know no one, no one knows them, no one looks like them? Who would sign up for that?

So part of my job, Roberta, has been to make sure that at every step of the way, they feel supported. This catalogue does not support those students.

ROBERTA. But –

SHERRI. Let. Me. Finish.

I counted this time. There are fifty-two photos in this catalogue. Do you know how many feature students of color? Do you?

ROBERTA.	SHERRI.
But I don't –	Three.

SHERRI. Three photos. Out of fifty-two. That's…

(She opens her desk drawer, grabs a calculator.)

That is 5.76 percent. I'll round up for you – that's six percent.

Our students of color? Who actually do go here? Represent eighteen percent.

(Quick beat.)

This is a failure, Roberta. An absolute failure.

(Beat.)

Why can't you make this work? *What* is the problem here?

(Beat.)

ROBERTA. I am doing the best job I can, Sherri.

SHERRI. I beg to differ.

ROBERTA. I worked very very hard on this catalogue –

SHERRI. I don't doubt that –

ROBERTA. And this is just one of a hundred different tasks on my plate. My plate – I have a very full plate!

SHERRI. So do I. So do we all.

ROBERTA. I don't see color. Maybe that's my problem. I'm not a race person. I don't look at race.

SHERRI. Let's agree to disagree about that, ok?

ROBERTA. You're the one who seems to care about race – you're always race race race, you never –

SHERRI. This isn't about me always ra– This – This is about me telling you what I need and continually being ignored!

ROBERTA. I don't ignore you! There are – I don't even believe you, because I do make an effort, since we talked, and I don't –

> (**SHERRI** *turns her computer around to the open document of the draft for the catalogue.*)

SHERRI. Here's the proposed cover photo: our boys lacrosse team. All white. Next: a photo of Dr. Fitzgerald, also white, talking to a white student. Next: a classroom where Ms. Morgan, also white, is teaching, and we see the back of three heads, again: all white.

ROBERTA. That one on the left could be Asian.

> (**SHERRI** *shoots her a look.*)

It's just the back of his head. It's black hair. You don't know.

SHERRI. Next: Mr. Mollizerri, white, standing in front of the white accompanist, teaching chorus to two students, also white. Next: three of our boys basketball players, including my son, which I do appreciate, but again, all white.

ROBERTA. No. No! That's Perry. That's Perry!

SHERRI. Roberta, please.

ROBERTA. Perry's Black! His father's Black! Don is Black –

SHERRI. Don is, is – biracial and Perry... he doesn't always photograph – he looks whiter than my son in this picture.

ROBERTA. But Perry's Black. Isn't he?

SHERRI. Of course he is but he doesn't read Black in this photo, that's the issue.

ROBERTA. But you count him as Black? In your statistics?

SHERRI. What?

ROBERTA. When you tell everyone we're eighteen percent, jumping for joy, eighteen percent, you're including Perry in that, aren't you?

SHERRI. A Black child, seeing this photo, does not see a reflection of himself. He sees three White boys.

ROBERTA. If Perry's Black, he's Black. If he's not, he's not. But I don't see how I'm not doing my job when I use a photo of a Black kid who everyone else at this school counts as Black, but when I count him as Black, he doesn't count as Black anymore. I just don't understand that.

    (Beat.)

SHERRI. I guess, Roberta, I guess my question for you is, do you not care if this school is diverse? Does that not matter to you?

ROBERTA. I don't like – what are you accusing me of here?

SHERRI. I'm not accusing you of anything, I'm asking you a question. Because it seems to me, year after year, you thwart my efforts to –

ROBERTA. I don't thwart anything Sherri I just don't have this same fixation on race as you do.

SHERRI. If no one fixated on it, nothing would ever change!

    (Breath.)

Look. Either you're on board with helping this department, or you're not, in which case, we have a problem.

ROBERTA. I'm *on board*, but all that comes out of your mouth is diversity, diversity, diversity. It's exhausting. Diversity of admissions, diversity is the theme of half the assemblies, diversity of – Until the day I die I won't forget the faculty meeting where you railed against the ethno-centric meal plan.

SHERRI. I don't think I railed, Roberta –

ROBERTA. Kids like pizza. Period. They don't care what continent it comes from, and it doesn't make the kitchen staff racist for serving pizza.

SHERRI. I never said anyone was racist for serving pizza.

ROBERTA. You certainly implied it, and Janine was very upset. She was in tears. She works so hard, trying to accommodate a hundred different demands: gluten-free pizza for the gluten-frees, vegetarian pizza for the vegetarians, lactose pizza for those kinds. She tries so hard, and then you call her a racist –

SHERRI. I never called her a racist!

ROBERTA. My family has been part of this school for almost a century. My father taught chemistry here for thirty-three years –

SHERRI. *(On "thirty-three.")* Thirty-three years, I know.

ROBERTA. No one loves this place more than I do, but sometimes I don't recognize this school anymore.

SHERRI. Maybe that's a good thing.

ROBERTA. I try and see people for who they are, I don't stop to examine the exact color of their skin the way you do. Last time you said more people of color, and that's what I tried to do, but apparently they were the wrong shade. So what do you want, Sherri? More dark-skinned ones?

SHERRI. Did you really just say dark-skinned?

ROBERTA. Isn't that what you're asking for?!?

SHERRI. What I am asking for is pictures of students who are recognizably minorities. So that another minority student can RECOGNIZABLY RECOGNIZE someone who looks like them.

ROBERTA. So you mean dark-skinned?

SHERRI. No that is not what I mean.

ROBERTA. Well then what exactly do you mean? You never say what you mean. Maybe if you were specific about what you want, I could do my job.

SHERRI. Ok. Fine. Let me be specific. I want to see a lot more – a significant increase in the number of photos of Black and Hispanic students. I want those students to be easily and readily identifiable as Black or Hispanic. Got it? And let's stay away from any sports photos.

ROBERTA. What's wrong with sports?

SHERRI. Nothing's wrong with sports, let's just focus on a broader range of images.

ROBERTA. Can you be more specific?

SHERRI. Some classroom shots. Holding up a glass beaker. Punching numbers into a calculator. Reading a book in English class.

ROBERTA. Does it matter which book, or any book will do?

SHERRI. Any book will do.

ROBERTA. Does it matter which class, or...

(**SHERRI** *thinks.*)

SHERRI. Why don't you try Don's class.

ROBERTA. So Don counts? He's Black enough?

SHERRI. Would you talk that way if Don were here with us right now?

ROBERTA. What's wrong with how I'm talking? I'm just trying to understand. I like Don. I'm happy to go to his class. He teaches junior English. That's when they do Moby Dick.

SHERRI. They don't read Moby Dick anymore.

ROBERTA. Sure they do. I remember, my brother, when he was a junior here, that was the year he read Moby Dick.

SHERRI. They don't read Moby Dick anymore.

(*Beat.*)

ROBERTA. You didn't.

SHERRI. We did. It's 2015. It's about time they realized not every book was written by a dead white man.

ROBERTA. Who cares who wrote the book, it's one of the great books.

SHERRI. There are plenty of other great books.

ROBERTA. But Moby Dick is a tough book, they'll never pick it up on their own.

SHERRI. Oh well.

ROBERTA. The poor children.

SHERRI. They're going to be alright.

>   (*Beat.*)

ROBERTA. Must be nice, to be so sure you're right, all the time.

SHERRI. I never said I was right *all* the time. But on this matter, I am. And I do run Admissions, and as long as I do, and as long as you work here, you'll do what I ask. Period.

>   (*Beat.*)

ROBERTA. This is going to take some time to redo.

SHERRI. I understand.

ROBERTA. Is that all?

SHERRI. Yes, Roberta. That's all.

ROBERTA. Ok then. More diversity, coming right up.

>   (*She stands up and puts on her coat. Then her scarf, then her hat, then her gloves. It takes fucking forever, which is incredibly awkward and frustrating for* **SHERRI**. *Then* **ROBERTA** *exits.*)

(Early that evening. In Sherri's open kitchen/ living room. A long staircase leads to the upstairs. **GINNIE** *sits at a barstool.)*

GINNIE. Shouldn't she have retired by now?

SHERRI. She'll never retire. She'll outlast us all. Roberta Russert and the cockroaches.

GINNIE. She is so white.

SHERRI. I know, I know.

GINNIE. This whole place is so white, *still*! Drives me insane. Ugh. If I were a terrorist, I'd blow this whole place right up.

SHERRI. Oh, don't do that.

GINNIE. I swear, as soon as I get Perry off to school, I'm gonna join the admissions committee.

SHERRI. She actually – by the end I actually had to say to her, MORE BLACK PEOPLE. MORE HISPANIC PEOPLE. DO YOU UNDERSTAND?

GINNIE. Screw her! She can't find any Black people here to photograph? Has she met my Black husband? Has she met my Black son? How! Lazy! Can! She! Be!

SHERRI. Oh no, she had a photo of Perry.

GINNIE. Well that's a start, right.

SHERRI. Yeah but he, he didn't...

(Quick beat.)

It was blurry. It was – it was kind of blurry.

GINNIE. Well, I've only got like a million photos of Perry, I'll send you some.

SHERRI. That'd be great.

GINNIE. I actually probably do have a million photos of him, it's stupid –

(Her phone dings with a text. She runs to it and checks.)

It's just Don. It's just Don. Oh god! Don!

*(***SHERRI*** *laughs.)*

This is what I mean, though. This is what I was telling you. I've been like this all day. What a nightmare! I mean, *Yale*? Why'd our boys apply to *Yale*? Who gets into Yale?

SHERRI. Oh, they definitely still take at least six out of a thousand.

GINNIE. *Six* out of a *thousand*?

SHERRI. *(Laughing.)* It's not quite that dire, but close.

GINNIE. Oh my god, what a nightmare.

All summer long, I begged him: apply to Middlebury. Cause, you know, his aunt is a dean there – my brother's wife, a total pill but, well-established, been there for years –

SHERRI. Right.

GINNIE. Apply to Middlebury. It's a *great* school, he loves to ski, and not for nothing but my *brother's wife* is a *dean* there. But Perry didn't want to do anything Charlie wasn't and Charlie was dead-set on Yale, which, in theory sounds fun, how fun does that sound, you and me, road trips to visit the boys at Yale doesn't that sound *fun* but *Yale*? Why Yale?

SHERRI. Because. Mystic Pizza.

GINNIE. Mystic Pizza?

SHERRI. The movie. You know –

GINNIE. That's a movie, right?

SHERRI. We used to watch over and over –

GINNIE. That's Julia Roberts?

SHERRI. A young Julia Roberts, yeah, and one of the girls goes to Yale and Charlie had such a crush on her. She was into astronomy, we bought Charlie a telescope, I thought that'd be the end of it, but he wanted the Yale sweatshirt, too. At *eight*. Ever since, Yale has been built up as...

(She builds a mountain with her hands and takes it all the way up to heaven. To God.)

GINNIE. Well call me crazy but I don't think childhood dreams should cost sixty thousand dollars a year I just don't.

SHERRI. Tell me about it. Maybe I can harvest an organ. How much does a kidney get you these days?

GINNIE. Less than what you and Bill make. You guys'll be fine.

SHERRI. I don't know. We took a real hit in the downturn.

GINNIE. Bill's Head of the School. You're Head of Admissions. You'll – you're gonna be fine!

SHERRI. And then my dad, all those trials he went on, before he – none of them were covered… The struggle is real, as the kids say.

GINNIE. Well, that's why there's cake.

SHERRI. Cake?

GINNIE. Oh, I have no brain today – yes, that's why I came over. Yes. I brought a cake. I, I was losing my mind at home, I didn't know what to do, so I went to Martin's Bakery. I don't know. I just thought, Perry's worked so hard, if he gets in, we'll celebrate, and if not, well, there's cake! And while I was there, I thought, let me pick one up for Charlie too, why not. Cake for everyone!

SHERRI. That was very sweet.

GINNIE. I hope Charlie likes carrot cake, it's Perry's favorite –

SHERRI. I'm sure he will.

GINNIE. I don't care what anyone says, Martin molested that child but it's Perry's favorite cake, what are you gonna do.

SHERRI. It's so sweet of you, Ginnie.

GINNIE. Yeah…

> (**SHERRI** *checks her phone again.* **GINNIE** *sees her do it.*)

Charlie's a great student, Sherri. He's on *basketball*, he's on the *paper*, he –

SHERRI. Yeah but, he's not Editor-in-Chief.

GINNIE. So?

SHERRI. It makes a difference.

GINNIE. You think?

SHERRI. Associate Editor's not bad but, it's not Editor-in-Chief it's just not.

GINNIE. Associate Editor is nothing to sneeze at!

SHERRI. And I get it. The paper hadn't had a female Editor since... I can't even remember?

GINNIE. Why don't girls ever want to be Editor? It's writing! Girls are good at that.

SHERRI. So when Olive Opatovsky showed interest, what could Jerry do? She's qualified, and it's been too long. I get it, I do, he had to pick Olive. But Charlie would have been –

GINNIE. He would have been excellent.

SHERRI. Thank you. And like I said, it's no one's fault, Charlie just happened to be in the same class as Olive Opatovsky, that's that. Them's the breaks. But...

GINNIE. Has there ever been a Black Editor-in-Chief?

SHERRI. Uhh... yes. Of course. Of – Marshall Washington.

GINNIE. *(Simultaneously.)* Marshall Washington. God, of course, yes. What's he up to now?

SHERRI. He went to Harvard, then Harvard Law, clerked for Ginsburg, and then he went –

GINNIE. Ruth Bader Ginsburg?

*(**SHERRI** nods and keeps talking.)*

SHERRI. He went to some big-shot law firm in New York, I'm told he does very well for himself, Bill met with him maybe two years ago? He couldn't get ten cents from Marshall.

GINNIE. You don't say?

SHERRI. Not ten cents. We were trying to start this thing for alumni of color but, when Bill explained it would also entail at least a small donation? Well. That was the end of that.

It's just – He's making all that money, sitting in his fancy office, a view apparently of the Statue of Liberty, and he's completely lost sight of the fact that he is where he is because of *us*. Because *we* took a chance on him. No gratitude. No gratitude at all.

> (**GINNIE** *says nothing. Then her phone rings. She answers it.*)

GINNIE. Hello? Perry. You –

> (*She moves just offstage into another room, for privacy.*)

Oh my god. Oh my god. Honey! Oh my god. I'm shaking. I'm –

You what? You can talk to your mother for two sec– tell Coach you need two seconds – tell Coach to hang on! Just –

Ok, fine, go, go, I'll see you soon. I got you a cake! Oh my god –

> (*Perry hangs up.* **GINNIE** *returns. The women scream.*)

SHERRI. I am so proud of him, that's wonderful.

GINNIE. Yale? Yale!

SHERRI. So well deserved. SO well deserved.

(Later that night.)

(BILL enters, having just come from outside, still wearing a coat. He drops his keys on the counter.)

SHERRI. He still hasn't called.

BILL. No?

SHERRI. And now his phone's off. Where'd you go?

BILL. Did you text him?

SHERRI. Only a hundred times.

BILL. So you haven't heard anything?

SHERRI. *(Shaking her head no.)* Where'd you go?

BILL. The gym, the library, he wasn't –

SHERRI. Did you check Gates Hall?

BILL. I checked the –

SHERRI. Did you check Gates Hall?

BILL. I didn't see him, Sher.

SHERRI. What about the dorms? Maybe he went – cause he sometimes likes to go with – did you check the –

BILL. I drove all over campus, I drove into town, I didn't see him.

SHERRI. I'm starting to get worried.

(Quick beat.)

I'm worried.

BILL. He's a grown man, if he –

SHERRI. He's seventeen! He's not a grown man. He's a boy –

BILL. Please don't yell at me.

SHERRI. I'm not yelling at you, I just –

BILL. You're yelling at me.

(Breath.)

SHERRI. It's... it's snowing out.

BILL. There are maybe, three flurries. Four, maybe.

SHERRI. And it's almost nine o'clock. I think we should call the police.

BILL. We don't need to call the police. Let's just relax.

SHERRI. What if he did something rash? What if he's thinking of doing something rash? What if he's about to do –

BILL. He's not going to *kill* himself if he didn't get into Yale.

SHERRI. Stranger things have happened. I think we should call the police.

BILL. He's a young man, if he's upset, if he – he's off somewhere cooling off, or, blowing off steam, or – whatever he's doing, he'll be fine. Let's just relax.

(*He goes over to the cake Ginnie left.*)

What is this? You got a cake?

SHERRI. Ginnie brought it.

(**BILL** *picks at the cake.*)

Don't pick at it. How can you eat?

BILL. I didn't eat all day. I'm hungry.

SHERRI. I didn't have time to make – I'm sor– I was frazzled –

BILL. That's ok.

SHERRI. Don't you want something more subst– shouldn't we wait for Charlie?

BILL. I'm hungry. Did you eat?

SHERRI. I can't.

BILL. You should eat something.

SHERRI. Well I can't, Bill. I'm –

(**CHARLIE** *bursts in through the front door.*)

Where have you been?

(**CHARLIE** *storms past his parents, runs up the stairs.*)

Charlie? Charlie?

(*We hear his door slam.* **SHERRI** *makes her way to the stairs.*)

BILL. Don't.

SHERRI. Charlie Luther Mason.

> *(She charges up the stairs.)*

BILL. Sherri.

> *(He remains downstairs. We hear* **SHERRI** *upstairs. She knocks on Charlie's door.)*

SHERRI. *(Offstage.)* Charlie, can I talk to you?

CHARLIE. *(Offstage.)* Please go away.

SHERRI. *(Offstage.)* I'd like to talk to you.

CHARLIE. *(Offstage.)* Please go away please. Thank you.

SHERRI. *(Offstage.)* No Charlie I'm not going away. I want to talk to you.

> *(She keeps knocking.)*

CHARLIE. *(Offstage.)* Can you stop? CAN YOU STOP?

> *(We hear him open the door.)*

Oh my god why are you so annoying.

SHERRI. *(Offstage.)* I want to talk to you. Charlie.

> *(***CHARLIE** *runs down the stairs, followed by his mother. He's heading out again.)*

BILL. Where do you think you're going?

CHARLIE. Leave me alone.

SHERRI. Do not walk out that door. You are not to walk out that door don't you dare walk out that door so help me God.

CHARLIE. What do you want from me?

SHERRI. Where have you been all night?

CHARLIE. Out. Ok?

SHERRI. No not ok. Out where?

CHARLIE. Just out.

SHERRI. It's snowing out!

CHARLIE. No it's not!

SHERRI. Come here I want to smell you.

CHARLIE. Mom will you just fucking back the fuck off? I'm not *hiiigh*. Ok. Back off.

SHERRI. Charles. Sit. Down.

CHARLIE. It's not even nine. I wasn't even out late. Can everyone just chill out? Jesus!

SHERRI. It is nine o'clock on a school night. Last time I checked you don't just stay out 'til nine o'clock on school nights. We texted you a hundred times, we called a hundred times, you didn't respond.

CHARLIE. My phone died.

SHERRI. Where were you?

CHARLIE. I was out in the woods. Screaming.

SHERRI. Screaming?

CHARLIE. Yes, screaming.

SHERRI. You're all red, you must be freezing.

CHARLIE. It's global warming, it's not that cold.

SHERRI. It's still December!

BILL. Where were you Charlie?

CHARLIE. I was in the woods, I'm not lying.

SHERRI. You went out in the woods to scream? For four hours?

CHARLIE. Yes. And then there was like, a deer, I was staring at it for a while, I don't know, I lost track of time.

BILL. Why did you go out into the woods to scream for four hours?

CHARLIE. Because I'm angry, ok? I'm angry, I'm frustrated, I'm upset, I'm upset.

SHERRI. Because of Yale, I presume?

CHARLIE. Correct, *Mother*. You *presume* correctly. Your *presumptions* are correct.

SHERRI. Were you rejected, or deferred?

CHARLIE. Deferred. Ok? Can we stop with the interrogation now?

SHERRI. *(On "interrogation.")* Ok well that – that *sucks*, but you still have a shot – you're still in this, it just means the process is going to take –

CHARLIE. Can you actually spare me your process lecture, I'm well aware of what the process entails, thank you.

SHERRI. I'm sorry, baby. Come here. You worked your tail off, you worked so hard, and I know how much you – It's a crapshoot.

CHARLIE. Is it, actually?

I feel so... *stupid*. I feel –

SHERRI. No!

CHARLIE. It's so –

SHERRI. What happened?

CHARLIE. It's so – I'm sorry, but it's *so* unfair, it's *so unfair* –

SHERRI. Are you upset because... Perry got in?

CHARLIE. How'd you know that?

SHERRI. Ginnie was here, when she got the –

CHARLIE. Can we not talk about that fucking birdbrain tonight?

SHERRI. Charlie!

CHARLIE. Sorry but she acts like it's this huge achievement that a not totally white baby popped out of her vagina –

SHERRI. Charlie!

CHARLIE. That's not actually an achievement! Just so you know!

SHERRI. Charlie. What happened?

What happened?

CHARLIE. What happened is, there we are at basketball, on a five, and Perry finds out he got into Yale, and everyone's like oh my god, so awesome man, so great man, fuck yeah man, you're the man, man, who's the fucking man, Perry's the fucking man. So I check my phone and there it is:

Dear Charles, delighted to consider you for admission, so many qualified candidates, record number applications, blah blah blah skim skim skim: We regret to inform you.

As if – like – I don't think an institution can have feelings of regret, I don't think that's how regret works, but...

I read the email, I read it again, and then I realize everyone's gotten really quiet. I turn around, and they're all staring at me, waiting for me to share my news. Everyone knew Perry and I both applied to Yale, everyone saw him get in, everyone heard him call his mother, I'm standing there holding my phone, everyone knows what I'm looking at, I couldn't get away. I was trapped, and so I had to be like: deferred.

And everyone stayed really quiet, and then it was like, all the air just got sucked out of the place, and you could feel every single person feeling the exact same thing:

How the FUCK did Perry Peters get into Yale and Charlie Mason get deferred?

This is a small school. Everyone knows everything about everyone. And I literally know Perry better than anyone. I know him, we grew up together since we were three, we're best friends, I know everything about him, I know him. And he's a good student, he is, he is, but his grades are not better than mine. His SAT scores are not better than mine. I actually do like a million more extracurriculars, he just does that like computer science club which isn't even a club and basketball and baseball, and we're basically equally good, he's like a little better at baseball I'm a little better at basketball but neither of us is getting recruited anytime soon, I take three APs he only takes two and, and maybe he did like *ten extra hours* during Stockings with Care but, that doesn't get you into *Yale*... And I just thought like, how did I not see this coming?

SHERRI. See what coming?

CHARLIE. That it was never – It was always about – Even that weekend we toured colleges with his family? A couple times it was just you me Perry and Ginnie, and when Perry's with his mom, you can't, you can't always tell, but when *Don* was with us, and Perry stood next to *him*... All those admissions officers who all had that same vague phony bullshit persona suddenly, like, came alive. They looked at him more, made more eye contact, were just a little more interested in every word that came out of his mouth, laughed harder than they needed to at every dumb thing he said, feeling so proud of themselves, so smug, they're changing the world on the daily and it was like, I AM STANDING RIGHT. HERE. I AM A HUMAN BEING JUST LIKE HIM AND I AM STANDING RIGHT HERE.

SHERRI. It's gonna be ok, sweetie.

CHARLIE. Can you honestly spare me your liberal guilty white bullshit for two seconds and hear what I'm saying?

I have been dealing with this like non-stop for like, the last two years. I mean, the whole Olive Opatovsky thing. I mean, that was some BULLSHIT. That was BULLSHIT.

SHERRI. Do you really want to rehash Olive Opatovsky again?

CHARLIE. The only reason she is Editor-in-Chief, the ONLY reason –

SHERRI. I guess so –

CHARLIE. Is because of fucking Joanna Feldstein, because Joanna Feldstein wrote that fucking letter.

"Every year, I wait, hoping a woman will *finally* ascend to the top ranks of the newspaper, and every year, I watch as yet another white man is named Editor-in-Chief."

As if there's, like, some mass conspiracy at the Hillcrest Student Newspaper, but what do you know? Two weeks after Joanna's letter, Dr. Fitzgerald announces the next Editor of the paper is: Olive Opatovsky. And now, not only are the editorials not as good as they could have been, but I got fucked. Just me. Just me. Olive and I were the only ones who even applied to be Editor. And last night, she got into Cornell. So...

SHERRI. Oh honey, if you'd applied to *Cornell* you would have gotten in, that's a no-brainer –

CHARLIE. You should have seen it, fucking, fucking Mrs. Dawson walked by the newspaper room and gave like the Rosie the Riveter arm to Olive, with this huge shit-eating grin on her face, and then we were walking to the vending machines and Mr. Brodsky high fives her and said, he literally said, "You go girl." Like, *what*? Why are we all pretending Olive somehow got this position cause she deserved it? I mean, don't we all know the truth?

(Very quick beat.)

BILL. Maybe the truth is, she got the position cause she's a better writer.

CHARLIE. *What?*

BILL. You have to at least entertain that possibility, don't you?

SHERRI. Bill, that is not helpful.

BILL. *(Stunned laughter.)* Oh, ok!

CHARLIE. She's a terrible writer, Dad! She's terrible!

BILL. Says who? Huh? Says who?

CHARLIE. Says me! Says anyone with eyes! Says anyone who can read – That's not what this is about, that's not why she got the job, and that's not an opinion, that's a fact.

BILL. Ok, let's *pretend* your facts are actually facts, and you're a better writer. In that case, what if Dr. Fitzgerald thought Olive would be a better leader.

CHARLIE. Olive is a horrible leader, Dad, she's horrible – she sits at these meetings at the head of the table, chewing on her sweatshirt, which is disgusting, like:

"I don't know who should write the story. I can't decide. You decide."

That's leadership? That's fucking leadership?

BILL. Do you want to hear what someone else has to say, or do you want to just keep listening to the sound of your own voice?

(Quick beat.)

Maybe having Olive serve as Editor is important for a number of reasons. Maybe it sends a message to Olive that she has leadership capabilities she might not have realized had someone not given her the chance to lead. Or maybe Olive already had qualities that we don't always associate with leadership but that are equally valuable and worthy. Maybe just having Olive as Editor lets other girls on the paper know that this is possible for them, and changes how they think of themselves, in this moment, and forever after. And maybe, it forces everyone in the school to look at the top positions of... anything, corporations, presidents, whatever, it impresses upon them right from the start that women belong in positions of power, that women are capable of being leaders, that –

CHARLIE. How does it help when she's a terrible writer?

BILL. That is your opinion, Charlie!

CHARLIE. No, that's a fact.

BILL. I'm sorry, but I would hardly call what's-his-face who was the Editor last year –

CHARLIE. Maurice.

BILL. Maurice, yes. I seem to recall many a dinner conversation where we were informed of what an incompetent writer Maurice was.

CHARLIE. He was! He was awful. It was painful. But no one else applied. There was literally no one else. I will grant you, if Olive had gone up against Maurice, I would have been first in line to make Olive Editor. She's fucking, she's Toni Morrison next to him. But – and I recognize how absurd it is for me to be like, objective about myself, but objectively speaking, *I'm* Toni Morrison next to Olive. Of COURSE a woman should run the newspaper. IF SHE'S THE BEST CANDIDATE. And in four years, that's just not how it shook out. Sorry Joanna.

BILL. Maybe. Or maybe there are larger forces at work. Maybe it's not random that one of the most prestigious positions for a student has not gone to a woman.

CHARLIE. You're not on the paper! You have no idea!

BILL. No, you're right Charlie, you're absolutely right, I see what you mean. We should just throw up our hands and let *white guys* run the show, that's definitely the better choice.

CHARLIE. Dr. Fitzgerald runs the show. At the paper? He runs the show. If it's so goddamn important for little girls to see women in power, then why doesn't he step aside and let a woman be the faculty advisor? Oh no no no no. No his solution is to just suddenly get super self-righteous about having a woman editor because it's fucking easy to make room at a table you don't have to sit at. Well, news flash from the people trying to sit at those tables: you can't just keep pulling up chairs. There isn't unlimited room. That's like, not how tables work. So let him go make room at his own table, leave mine alone!

(Beat.)

I am drowning over here, ok? I am – Because I am not one of those – I get that there are entitled white men who assume they get a seat without having to do anything to earn it, I do go to Hillcrest after all, and I do have eyes, but I'm actually one of the people working really fucking hard to earn a seat, and every time I get close it's like, ew! Not *you*! No one wants *you* here, fuck off. And it's all. I. Hear. I mean, fucking Joanna Feldstein, in English last week, we're reading *Willa Cather* who is not only a woman but was also like, basically a lesbian, and Joanna was like, it is *soul crushing* to read so many white books, why can't we ever read anything by people of color, and I was like, first of all, we barely ever read books by white people anymore, thanks to my parents actually, but also, YOU'RE WHITE JOANNA. So what are you talking about? Do you hate yourself? You say white like you hate yourself. Because, I'm not an idiot, I don't have white pride, but I don't *hate* myself. And then Cristobal Hernandez was like, I'm also sick of all these white books and I was like, Cristobal! YOU'RE

WHITE TOO! And he was like, are you fucking kidding me? And I was like, NO! I'M NOT! Look in a mirror. You're white. You're from Chile. Who is from Chile who's white? Indigenous people weren't white, African slaves weren't white, if you're white, that means your ancestors were colonizers, not the colonized, that's like the only way you end up white unless you're albino and you don't seem albino to me, and Joanna was like, maybe you could shut up and listen for once and I was like I do listen, all the time, but also, class participation is a huge part of my grade so if I don't speak, it actually hurts my chances of getting into a good college cause I don't have any special boxes to check, so sorry if the sound of my voice is so upsetting but I actually have no choice I have to talk my whole future depends on it. At which point Priscilla Chen agreed with *me*, so Cristobal turned on her and I was like, hold up. Priscilla's dad is an immigrant from Taiwan. *Your* dad is a *Chilean ambassador* who's clearly descended from a bunch of white people, but when Priscilla applies to college she goes in the shit pile too, cause Asian people are actually dealing with a whole bunch of quotas right now, but maybe you'd like to explain why you would be *thrilled* if we replaced Willa Cather with an Asian writer, but if that Asian writer has a kid applying to college, then everyone suddenly stops caring that that kid is a person of color. And by the way, who even decides? Cause I would really like to meet the person who decides who counts as a person of color and who doesn't and who's white and who's not, and who's Asian and who's like descended from the continent of Asia but isn't supposed to call themselves Asian cause like, Armenia's in Asia and Kim Kardashian's half Armenian so is Kim Kardashian a woman of color, or do you have to be from specific countries in Asia to say you're Asian and if you're from other countries in Asia where people look sorta white, then do we just call you white? Who makes that decision? And what about Black people? Do they all just check one box called Black cause I'd be curious to know how Rwandans feel about that cause, call me crazy but doesn't it stand to reason that if a group of people commit a genocide against another group of people, the victims of that genocide probably don't ever want to be lumped into the same category as their killers, at least, not for a while, right? And can someone please tell me, is Penélope Cruz a person of color, cause she's from Spain but she speaks Spanish, and so if she *is* of color then are we saying all people from Spain are of color? And if all people from Spain are of color, then why not French people, or Italian people? They're all right there on the Mediterranean, what is so special about Spain? Like, if Penélope Cruz is a person of color then I think we should discuss why Sophia Loren and Marion Cotillard are not. But if Penélope Cruz is *not* a person of color, then can someone tell me why a *white* lady with *Spanish* blood who lives in *Spain* is *white*; but a *white* lady with *Spanish* blood who lives in *Argentina* is *not white*. WHO DECIDES. Because if you're gonna sit there and tell me you want to read more books by people of color, then you better explain to me what a person of color is, and like, why I'm not one of them, cause my mom's dad had to escape before like half his family was murdered by Nazis, but now when we all apply to college, I go in the shit pile too, even though my grandfather couldn't get into an Ivy League seventy years ago because they had super intense quotas against Jews, but – shocker! – they found a new way to keep Jews out: they just made us white instead, and now the grandsons of Nazis who came to America go in the exact same pile as me, which makes absolutely no sense, and the grandsons of Nazis who ran away to South America go in an EVEN BETTER PILE, which makes EVEN LESS SENSE, alongside you, Cristobal Hernandez, direct descendant of murderous, genocidal Spanish conquistadors, but I tell you what, I bet my grandfather's cousins would've given anything to be Spanish conquistadors instead of corpses in Auschwitz. But keep pushing me keep fucking pushing me go

sit at whatever fucking table you want while you tell
me how white I am and how disgusting I am, I'll just
stand in the corner taking it all in until I can't fucking
take it anymore and I all of a sudden break out into a
FUCKING SIEG HEIL!!!!!

 (He does the Sieg Heil, then drops his hand.)
 (Beat.)

SHERRI. Did you... you said that? In class?

 (Beat.)

BILL. *(Genuinely impressed.)* Wow. Wow.

 (Then:)

What a spoiled brat. Spoiled little overprivileged brat.

SHERRI. Bill!

BILL. If you could see what I see – if you could see yourself
right now. You've had it so hard? What the fuck did
you do? You did your fucking homework? You want
a parade? What a little shit. Mom and I busted *our*
asses to get jobs at a great institution so you could go
there *for free*. And because you didn't squander that
opportunity, the world should be your fucking oyster
now? Open your little snot-faced eyes and look around.
Life is not fair. It's miserably unfair, but it's not little
white boys in private schools in New England who have
it so bad. Look at Fortune 500 CEOs. Look at Congress.
Look at – White guys run everything. Everything. Why
is that Charlie? Is it because white men are genetically
predisposed to be geniuses? Use your fucking brain. So,
ok – so one overprivileged quarter-Black kid got into
Yale and one overprivileged white kid didn't. Stop the
presses! Little Charlie, who had the world handed to
him on a silver platter didn't get the caviar he ordered.
He's gonna have to settle for duck confit. So you didn't
get into Yale. So you'll go to Dartmouth. You'll go to
Duke. And you'll be fine. And you know how I know
you'll be fine? Because you're a white guy and you don't
have down syndrome. I'm not worried. So why don't

you take a look at how the world *actually* works, and trot on up those stairs and go think about what the fuck went wrong in your brain to turn you into a racist spoiled little shit. For shame.

> *(Quick beat. Then* **CHARLIE** *storms upstairs, slams his door.* **BILL** *and* **SHERRI** *watch him go, frozen. Then:)*

Well. It looks like we successfully raised a Republican. Go us.

What?

What?

SHERRI. I cannot believe how you just talked to him.

BILL. How *I* talked to *him*? Were you not just here for that hideous screed?

SHERRI. He's upset, Bill. He's upset.

BILL. That's what you would call that display? Upset?

SHERRI. He's hurting. He wanted something, he worked really hard for it and he didn't get it, and he's trying to understand why and it's not making sense to him. How do you not see that?

BILL. A lot of good kids didn't get into Yale tonight. Our son is not some anomaly. There is not some conspiracy afflicting our son and our son alone.

SHERRI. Ok relax. No one said there was a conspiracy, but he's entitled to his feelings.

BILL. What part of that racist, sexist screed is he entitled to?

SHERRI. I haven't found any of Olive's editorials to be particularly insightful –

BILL. It's a high school paper Sherri! It's not supposed to be insightful – Ok, I'm done talking about Olive Opatovsky. And FYI, I'm done pretending he's suddenly Jewish. When did that happen?

SHERRI. Well technically, he is. I'm a Jew.

BILL. Well I'm not, you're – *(Unspoken: not that Jewish.)* He's an atheist. He is a white atheist. Maybe he's just waking up to the fact that it's not exactly cool to be white, but latching onto your dead grandfather's Auschwitz cousins because you get deferred from Yale is kind of tasteless, if you ask me.

SHERRI. I didn't ask you. But he's supposed to forge his own path. Maybe he doesn't want to be an atheist. I don't know. He's supposed to rebel. That's what kids do. It's what we did.

BILL. We rebelled against racist parents. We're not racist. So what's he rebelling against? Or what's he rebelling into? That's a scary thought.

SHERRI. My parents weren't racist.

BILL. Ok, I honestly don't have the patience to break down your parents' racism for you right now.

SHERRI. They weren't. They took me to march on Washington –

BILL. *(On "march.")* To march on Washington, I know, I know.

SHERRI. I named my son – we named our son Charlie *Luther* Mason.

BILL. And look how that turned out.

SHERRI. Wow Bill. Your compassion is, touching.

BILL. Oh, oh, oh, I should have more *compassion* for his point of view. Ok. Ok. Let's go dig the hole out front to lay the foundation for the pole so we can start flying the Confederate flag around here.

SHERRI. I happen to think Charlie was a stronger candidate.

BILL. That's because you're his mother.

SHERRI. No. That's me speaking objectively.

BILL. Well, objectively speaking, you've turned away plenty of Charlies for Perrys, and Cristobals, and the kids of wealthy white alum, wealthy siblings and legacies, even for a few of the boys on our football team. I've seen you do it, you do it all the time.

SHERRI. That is not what I do.

BILL. That's exactly what you do. You even have an award for it. You're Sherri Rosen-Mason, award-winning rejecter of white boys.

(Beat.)

BILL. Look: at the end of the day, he's gonna be fine. He's gonna be fine. Yale? Not Yale? Does it really matter?

SHERRI. Yeah, it really matters. We all sat around and looked it up when Charlie was filling out his application. Every single Supreme Court justice went to Harvard or Yale. The last four presidents all went to an Ivy League school.

BILL. Uhh, honey, I don't think Charlie has Supreme Court justice in his future. Or president. Hate to break it to you.

SHERRI. You don't know, but that's not the point. If you don't have a school like Yale or Harvard on your resume, that actually puts a ceiling on what's possible in your life. And our son is smart enough to see that. Going to Yale means your life contains all the possibility in the world. Not going there, or one of a handful of schools like it, means there are tables you will never get to sit at, tables whose existence you may never even know about. You're shut out before you even start freshman orientation. He's seventeen, he wants possibility in his life, and I want that for him, too.

(Beat.)

BILL. I'll make some calls tomorrow.

SHERRI. We have to know someone at Yale.

PART TWO: FEBRUARY

*(Sherri's office. **SHERRI** looks at her computer.*
ROBERTA *is with her.)*

SHERRI. Is this a joke?

ROBERTA. What do you mean? No, of course not. This is what you asked for.

SHERRI. This is not what I asked for.

ROBERTA. You told me I needed to put in more diversity...

SHERRI. There are NO white people in this mock-up. Having no white people is not diversity.

ROBERTA. So you're not happy?

SHERRI. Did you think I'd be happy?

ROBERTA. Last time I was here, you said more people of color.

SHERRI. This is not what Hillcrest looks like, it's not what we're selling. We're not trying to ERADICATE white people. We're trying to diversify. Diversify still means there are white people here.

ROBERTA. Just, fewer of them.

*(**SHERRI** slams her desk.)*

I really can't take much more of this, Sherri.

SHERRI. *You* can't take this?

ROBERTA. I worked my tail off on this, I mean, I worked *so* hard, and I show you the work I've done and you scream at me.

SHERRI. I am not *screaming* at you, Roberta –

ROBERTA. If you're not happy, you're not happy, but you could at least do me the courtesy of recognizing how hard I worked. I spent the last two months almost giving myself a nervous breakdown trying to give you what you wanted. I mean, just this one photo here, of the English class, I had to SCOUR the class rosters to find a section where there were even two Black kids in the same class. THAT ALONE took two days, pouring over every list, trying to remember who was Black, because I don't know all the students, not by name, I work in development, that's not my job. So I finally find a class with two Black kids, I work it out with the teacher, schedule the photographer, block out the time in my day, we show up, and what do you know? Stephanie is out sick. I'm standing there, like an idiot, making up some cockamamie excuse about why we can't take the photos even though we are standing in the middle of the classroom because I didn't think it was right to say, "We have to have two Black kids for this photo. One isn't enough." I didn't think I should say that. So, I reschedule with Mr. Matthews, reschedule the photographer, we come BACK a week later, and then Shemar is just looking down, the whole time, doodling or something, completely disengaged. So *I* had to interrupt and say, "Shemar, what did you think of *The Bluest Eye*?" So *two weeks* after I first scoured that list, we finally got the shot: Shemar talking, Stephanie behind him, holding up *The Bluest Eye* so you can see the cover... If that's not good enough for you, I give up!

SHERRI. No. I appreciate that. I appreciate – I understand, I do, I recognize that that took a lot of work. Getting the right photos, when the pool is so limited, it's... I understand how complicated that is. But now we've gone too far in the other direction. So we need to, let's tip it back. I love this shot of Shemar, and I love the shot you got of Alexis in chemistry, I love that, let's keep that, but there are too many now. And, to be totally honest, there are too many of the, of our students of co– of our students of color sitting together in the cafeteria. We don't want Hillcrest to look like it's segregated. Because it's not.

ROBERTA. The Black kids sit with the Black kids, Sherri, I didn't *ask* them to.

SHERRI. No, I know, *some* of them do, but some of them intermingle with other –

ROBERTA. I didn't see intermingling. And I looked. Believe me, I looked. I felt like David Duke: Where are the Black kids, where are the Black kids? There was a little intermingling but it wasn't the dark-skinned ones, so –

SHERRI. Ok! Ok! You know what? Then let's stage it. Ok? Let's stage it.

ROBERTA. Stage it?

SHERRI. Yes. We've done this before. We'll just get a group of students, and ask them to sit together, and we'll shoot some photos.

ROBERTA. Fine.

SHERRI. Ok, thank you.

ROBERTA. Which students?

SHERRI. Just, any nice assortment of diverse students –

ROBERTA. Uh uh uh. This is where I got in trouble last time. No. You pick 'em. You're the one who has to be happy, you pick 'em.

SHERRI. A diverse group, Roberta!

ROBERTA. I need specifics. I don't want to get this wrong. I don't have *time* to get this wrong. Which. Students.

(Beat.)

SHERRI. Alexis Whitmore. Uhm... Olive Opatovsky.

*(**ROBERTA** writes this down.)*

Wei-Lin Lee. Is he in the tenth grade now?

ROBERTA. I don't know I'll have to look.

SHERRI. Mark. Mark Goodman. Uhm... Danilo. Danilo Rodriguez. Uhm... who did I say so far?

ROBERTA. Alexis, Olive, Wei-Lin, Mark and Danilo. That's two whites, one Black, one Asian, one Hispanic.

SHERRI. Ok. Let's get, uhm, uhm... who's that new freshman, the one from India?

ROBERTA. I don't know.

SHERRI. Ok, I'll find out, but let's get her. And let's get two more. Uh... Madison Fiske. Let's get her. She's pretty. And... Tyler Robinson.

ROBERTA. That's three whites, two Blacks, one Hispanic, two Asian.

SHERRI. Thank you, Roberta.

ROBERTA. I don't know their religions. Or orientations –

SHERRI. That won't be necessary.

ROBERTA. So it's only the race we care about? Just so I'm clear?

SHERRI. Yes, Roberta.

ROBERTA. Ok well, this is gonna take me a little bit.

SHERRI. I understand.

ROBERTA. How do I find out who this Indian girl is?

SHERRI. Aparijita. Aparijita Patel.

ROBERTA. Apara what?

SHERRI. Aparijita.

      (Quick beat.)

ROBERTA. Can you spell that?

SHERRI. A-p-a-r-i –

ROBERTA. Slower.

SHERRI. A-p-a-r-i –

ROBERTA. A. P. A. R. I.

SHERRI. J-i-t-a.

ROBERTA. J. I. T. A.

SHERRI. Great. Thank you, Roberta.

ROBERTA. *(Slowly.)* Aparijita.

SHERRI. Yup.

      (Beat. Then **ROBERTA** *gets up to leave.)*

ROBERTA. I just wanted to say: I was sorry to hear Charlie didn't get into Yale.

SHERRI. Oh, it's – how'd you hear?

ROBERTA. It's a small school, Sherri. Everyone heard.

SHERRI. Oh. Right. Well, he was deferred, so, we'll see...

ROBERTA. Still, he's a really smart kid. He should've gotten in.

SHERRI. Thank you.

ROBERTA. But then I heard, Perry got in? That's a shame.

SHERRI. Why is that a shame?

ROBERTA. Because. Those boys are attached at the hip. I see them everywhere, always playing basketball. It would've been nice for them to go off to school together.

SHERRI. Oh. Yes, well...

ROBERTA. But I didn't see Charlie at the last game I went to, when was it, around Valentine's Day? Was he injured?

SHERRI. Oh, no, he's... he's not playing this year.

ROBERTA. Oh. That's too bad. What happened?

SHERRI. I'm not sure.

      (**ROBERTA** *smiles, then exits.*)

(Later. Sherri's house.)

*(**GINNIE** enters with a bakery box of cookies. She brings them to **CHARLIE**.)*

*(Behind them, **SHERRI** begins preparing dinner.)*

GINNIE. These are mini biscottis, these are mini cannolis. I don't know what these are called, I just love them –

SHERRI. Which ones?

GINNIE. The green trees with the chocolate inside. They're better when you scrape them on your teeth. Trust me. And these are rainbow cookies, which I say are tasteless but Perry says I'm wrong, these are totos, and these are Sicilian almond. So...

SHERRI. You baked all of those?

GINNIE. No, no. I picked them up at Martin's.

CHARLIE. The child molester?

GINNIE. Well, they never did prove anything, and he really does have the best –

SHERRI. It's really sweet of you, Ginnie.

GINNIE. Oh, it's nothing.

(Quick beat.)

SHERRI. *Charlie?*

CHARLIE. What – are – are these for me?

GINNIE. They're, they're not for – they're for all of you. They're... for all you guys.

CHARLIE. Thanks?

GINNIE. I was in the neighborhood. I was at Martin's, getting cookies for the team and, I remembered you're not – decided not to play, and I realized I wasn't gonna see you at the game and, I haven't seen you much lately and I missed, is all. So I thought I'd drop by. With cookies!

SHERRI. It's really thoughtful Ginnie.

GINNIE. We miss you, stranger.

CHARLIE. I've been pretty busy, so...

GINNIE. I can see that.

> *(She waits for **CHARLIE** to open up. He doesn't. She moves toward **SHERRI**.)*

And how are you? Miss Twenty Percent!!

SHERRI. Oh, how did you –

GINNIE. Don texted me, Bill told him today.

SHERRI. Did he?

GINNIE. Yeah. That is incredible. I mean, twenty percent!

SHERRI. We'll see, I have to scrounge up a whole other scholarship, who knows if I can even make –

GINNIE. Twenty percent! Wow! Yes!

> *(She high fives **SHERRI**.)*

Go Sherri go!

SHERRI. Not unless I get that scholarship – Charlie are you gonna want sour cream in your taco? I think this might have expired.

GINNIE. How'd you manage it?

SHERRI. What? Oh. Uhm, well… we're finally on the radar in China, we're seeing a lot more applications from –

GINNIE. Oh so it's just Asians driving up the numbers?

> *(A microscopic beat before **SHERRI** continues.)*

SHERRI. We got four applications from this charter school in the Bronx, and one girl applied from Saudi Arabia –

GINNIE. Wow.

SHERRI. We're finally starting to really get on the map in a real way, which is…

GINNIE. Amazing, absolutely amazing.

SHERRI. Yeah. So, we'll see.

GINNIE. Without you and Bill, I can't even imagine how *white* this place would still be. It makes my skin crawl to think about. I'm so proud of you, Sherri! Aren't you proud of your mom?

CHARLIE. I'm proud.

> *(He gets up to go. **SHERRI** watches him go.)*

GINNIE. Has this not been the craziest winter? I've been dragging this coat around like I even need it, I can't remember a February this warm. If this is what 2016 is like, what's it gonna be ten years from now?

SHERRI. That's a scary thought.

GINNIE. It's terrifying...

> *(Charlie's gone.)*

Is he ok?

SHERRI. He's... he's been feeling very sensitive, lately.

GINNIE. What's going on with him?

SHERRI. I don't know.

GINNIE. Why'd he quit basketball? I thought he loved playing on that team?

SHERRI. He's going through something, I –

CHARLIE. *(Offstage.)* I can hear you talking about me.

> **(SHERRI** *and* **GINNIE** *look at each other.* **CHARLIE** *comes back downstairs.)*

If you want to talk about me don't wait 'til I leave the room.

GINNIE. I was just asking your mom if everything's ok? Cause you seem down to me buddy.

CHARLIE. I'm not down.

GINNIE. Ok. Well. Good. Good.

SHERRI. Charlie, one taco or two?

CHARLIE. Three.

GINNIE. We miss you at those games. We could really use your three-pointers!

CHARLIE. I didn't get into college early, so, I still have to worry about my grades and everything.

GINNIE. Definitely. Definitely.

CHARLIE. Basketball just gets in the way...

GINNIE. I still have my fingers crossed for you about Yale. And my toes.

CHARLIE. Well, I don't, but, thanks.

GINNIE. A positive outlook is very important. That's what I always tell Perry.

CHARLIE. Yeah I don't think it was Perry's positive outlook that got him into Yale, but...

(Beat.)

See ya later.

(He goes upstairs. Beat. Then **SHERRI** *keeps chopping.)*

SHERRI. These tomatoes feel overripe, but that's ok in a taco, right?

GINNIE. Sure. Sherri?

SHERRI. Yeah?

GINNIE. What was that?

SHERRI. What was what?

GINNIE. Was Charlie... was he insinuating something? About Perry?

SHERRI. I didn't notice that.

GINNIE. Well. I sort of did. Actually. And, frankly, I'm surprised you didn't say anything. You just... let him.

SHERRI. He is... struggling to figure out where he fits into the world right now. Let's leave it at that.

GINNIE. Sherri.

SHERRI. What?

GINNIE. He just stood here and insinuated that Perry didn't deserve to get into Yale.

SHERRI. He didn't insinuate that –

GINNIE. And you let him say it.

SHERRI. I can't police what he says but no I don't think he –

GINNIE. You are his mother.

SHERRI. I'm well aware I'm his mother.

GINNIE. Kids don't just say things, is... I mean, is that indicative of what you and Bill say in this house, when we're not here, behind closed doors?

SHERRI. No. It's not. But he's not five, he doesn't just regurgitate what we say, he is an independent thinker. He speaks his mind freely.

GINNIE. Uh-huh. Uh-huh.

You don't know what Perry checked on his application. Maybe he didn't check anything. Maybe he left that part blank.

(Beat.)

SHERRI. Ginnie.

GINNIE. Yes Sherri?

(Beat.)

SHERRI. I'm going to start dicing an onion, if that's ok.

GINNIE. Is there something you want to say to me?

SHERRI. No.

GINNIE. Are you sure?

(Beat.)

SHERRI. It would surprise me if Perry hadn't checked Black.

GINNIE. Why would that *surprise* you?

SHERRI. Because it is a positive, it is beneficial, and he would have been foolish not to use anything he had at his disposal. Like any kid. Like all of them.

GINNIE. Right, but, I don't think that's what you were holding back from saying just now.

SHERRI. What is it you want to hear me say, exactly? That Perry couldn't have gotten into Yale without checking Black?

GINNIE. Is that how you feel?

SHERRI. I hope he did check Black! That's why those boxes exist, I believe in that! I've spent my whole life fighting for that.

GINNIE. And that's how you really feel?

SHERRI. That's how I really feel.

GINNIE. That's how you really feel?

SHERRI. That is how I really feel Ginnie.

GINNIE. So then you think –

SHERRI. Ginnie! You're not going to get me to say anything else on the matter. Ok?

(*Beat.*)

GINNIE. I'm gonna go. I'm feeling... I'm gonna go.

(*She begins to leave.*)

SHERRI. Ginnie... wait. Ginnie?

(*Beat.* **GINNIE** *stops, collects herself.*)

GINNIE. The next time your family's sitting around wondering why a Black kid got something a White kid didn't, maybe you could help me figure out this: Why does my husband have the same credentials as yours, and mine teaches English, and yours is Head of a School? Bill had the same experience as Don when he got here, but they took a big chance hiring Bill. How come no one's taken a chance like that on Don? He's applied to run schools. Great guy, they say, but not enough... experience. Work twice as hard, get half as far. What's that about? That's what we're trying to work out in my house. Excuse me.

(*She exits. After a moment,* **CHARLIE** *comes downstairs.*)

CHARLIE. Are you mad at me?

(*Beat.*)

SHERRI. Help me set the table.

CHARLIE. Mom?

SHERRI. What?

CHARLIE. Are you mad at me?

(*Beat. He sits near his mother.*)

SHERRI. I'm not mad at you, but, I think you need to take a good, hard look in the mirror, sweetie. You need to think very carefully about the kind of person you want to be in the world. Because, there are hateful people, and bitter people, and then there are people who, who

are trying to make a difference. You have to decide
what kind of person you want to be.

> *(Beat. After a moment, we hear the front door
> open.* **SHERRI** *turns.)*

BILL. *(Offstage.)* Hello hello.

SHERRI. Hi.

> (**BILL** *enters carrying a bottle of wine,
> humming "A bottle of red, a bottle of white,"
> and presents it to* **SHERRI**.)

What's this? Oh, this is nice. What's the occassio– Bill!

> (**BILL** *kisses her.)*

What is all this –

BILL. You. Are an incredible woman.

SHERRI. What is all of this?

BILL. Twenty percent? Twenty percent!

SHERRI. Oh. Oh. No –

BILL. No no no no no. This calls for a celebration. This is –

SHERRI. Bill, let's not –

BILL. Since you told me today, I am bursting, I can't stop
saying twenty percent. Twenty –

SHERRI. Bill we really don't need to go into this to–

> (**BILL** *gets wine glasses and pours at some
> point during the following.)*

BILL. Yes we do. Yes we do. You're too modest, you're always
so – but this doesn't just happen, it's not – the arc of
history doesn't naturally bend toward justice on its
own.

SHERRI. Oh my god Bill.

BILL. When you think about – when I think about, the
work, the fearless, tireless, intrepid work – the trips,
crisscrossing the country, to Boston, New York,
Philadelphia, to Baltimore, Newark – that winter you
got snowed in in Pittsburgh for five days – but there
she is, pounding the pavement, and the phone calls, the
emails, so many emails, the follow-ups, the follow-ups

to the follow-ups, the mentor program you started, the personal check-ins, what admissions officer does that, and who ever says, thank you?

SHERRI. I don't need to be thanked –

BILL. Twenty percent doesn't happen by chance, honey. It's a lifetime of work, and it's thankless work. But tonight – Charlie, you can have some too – tonight we are just going to take a second and take this in. I could not be prouder, I – it is not possible. Aren't you proud of Mom?

CHARLIE. *(Genuinely.)* I'm proud.

BILL. And, I know, your father would be, extraordinarily proud. Cheers.

SHERRI. *(Genuinely touched.)* Thanks.

> *(They cheers, all three of them.)*

BILL. *(Re: the wine.)* It's nice.

SHERRI. Excellent.

BILL. Remember the year we hit nine percent? Remember that? We thought we'd really done it. Twenty percent sounded like, landing someone on Mars would be easier.

SHERRI. I'm still one scholarship short, but –

BILL. I will find the money.

> (**SHERRI** *nods, then goes back to preparing dinner.*)

SHERRI. I'm a little behind, but...

BILL. There's no rush. What's tonight, taco night? Mmm.

> *(He takes a sip of wine.)*

You saw my email from John?

SHERRI. Uh, I don't know...

BILL. Thomas? Thomasson? I can't remember, just, be on the lookout.

SHERRI. Ok, great.

CHARLIE. For what?

BILL. What Charlie?

CHARLIE. Be on the lookout for what? Something from John... Watson? What, another application from the super rich friends of John Watson? Thomas? Thomasson?

Be on the lookout, Mom! Rich people are coming!

SHERRI. Thank you, Charlie. Why don't you go wash up for dinner?

(CHARLIE exits. BILL inspects the counter.)

BILL. And cookies, too! Tacos *and* cookies, wow.

SHERRI. Don't spoil your appetite.

(BILL eats a cookie. SHERRI approaches him.)

I think we shouldn't discuss applicants at home.

BILL. Why? We can trust Charlie, we've always talked about –

SHERRI. It's not about trust. He's – he can't handle it.

BILL. *Handle* it?

SHERRI. We will discuss what happened later, but –

BILL. What happened?

SHERRI. We will discuss it later –

BILL. What happened?

SHERRI. But suffice it to say, let's not talk about John Watson in front of him, or twenty percent, or any of it. Let's think up something... *fun* to discuss at dinner, please?

(Quick beat.)

BILL. We could talk about your brother.

SHERRI. Not funny.

BILL. It's a little funny.

SHERRI. Not funny.

BILL. We could talk about how beautiful you look.

SHERRI. That's ok.

BILL. There's a new town council proposal about a sewage waste facility they want to build?

SHERRI. Oh please God yes!

PART THREE: APRIL

(**SHERRI** *sits in her office, working.*)

(**CHARLIE** *pokes his head in.*)

CHARLIE. Hi Mom.

SHERRI. Hi honey. You have lunch yet?

CHARLIE. Yeah.

SHERRI. What'd you have?

CHARLIE. Pizza.

SHERRI. That's good. Is it raining out?

CHARLIE. A little. Drizzling.

SHERRI. April showers bring May flowers.

CHARLIE. Yeah.

Mom?

SHERRI. Yes.

CHARLIE. Can I talk to you a second?

SHERRI. Give me two...

(*She finishes up an email.* **CHARLIE** *fidgets.*)

Ok. What's up lovey?

CHARLIE. So. Ok. So. I have thoughts.

SHERRI. I have ears.

CHARLIE. So, I've been thinking about – so remember that night when I got deferred?

SHERRI. Yyyyyes.

CHARLIE. Yeah. I know. I've been thinking about that night a lot lately.

SHERRI. Ok.

CHARLIE. I hated how, like – the things I was saying? The words I was saying? That's not me.

SHERRI. I know that.

CHARLIE. I was like a crazy person that night.

SHERRI. You were upset. We all get upset. You used your words, which was good. A lot of people don't use words when they're upset. It's a sign of maturity.

CHARLIE. I went into the woods and screamed.

SHERRI. Screaming isn't a crime.

CHARLIE. And then I, like, I feel like I became obsessed with – I don't know. I just... That's not me. Or if it is, that's not who I want to be. That's not who I was raised to be. Because I'm not a conservative. I hate conservatives.

SHERRI. I know you do.

CHARLIE. And, I want to be the kind of person who makes a difference. I've been thinking about that a lot lately, actually.

SHERRI. Good. Good.

CHARLIE. And the more I think about, like, everything, the more I'm just... horrified.

SHERRI. What do you mean?

CHARLIE. I don't know. I... I was eating lunch the other week, with Eric and Chase, who I don't even like, but whatever, and we were talking about where everyone in our class applied to school and Eric was like, I still think it's so *unfair* you didn't get into Yale. And as he said *unfair*, he dipped like six French fries into this mound of ketchup, which he pours on his plate every day and then like throws out half of, and watching him shove French fries down his throat while he talked about what's fair...

SHERRI. Yeah.

CHARLIE. He wastes so much ketchup.

SHERRI. I hate that.

CHARLIE. Is it *fair* that Eric's dad went to Penn, made a bazillion dollars, and – shocker – Eric got in early to Penn? Is it *fair* that Chase's mom's best friend is on the board at Colby and now Chase is going to Colby? Cause intellectually speaking, Chase is about as gifted as defrosted meatloaf, but... Is it *fair* that *any time* John Watson's friends apply to Hillcrest he calls Dad for help?

What is fair? And who decides? Or is the definition of *fair* something a bunch of white guys made up right before they founded all the prep schools in the world?

(**SHERRI** *laughs.*)

I don't know if every student of color here is a genius, but I do know there's a shitton of idiot white kids sitting in that cafeteria, and I looked around, at everyone in that room, and thought about what had to happen, historically speaking, so each one of us could be sitting here, at this moment, in this elite space. And why, after everything you've done, it's still so white.

(*Beat.*)

We can't just sit around eating lunch, knowing something's not right and not do anything about it.

SHERRI. I agree.

CHARLIE. I knew you would. And that's why I go into that more in the... in the...

SHERRI. In the what?

(*Beat.*)

CHARLIE. I, uhm, I need to prepare you for something.

(*Beat.*)

SHERRI. Go. I'm listening.

CHARLIE. Ok. So. An editorial is coming out in today's paper, and I wrote it. And... it's kind of a big deal.

SHERRI. Ok...

CHARLIE. And like, it talks about how I did something, and like, it's kind of like, a big thing, that I did, and, like –

SHERRI. Not so many "likes" Charlie.

CHARLIE. Sorry. I'm nervous.

Ok. It's about something I did, and I don't want you to be upset or embarrassed if people ask you about it, so I'm telling you, so you know about it before the paper comes out.

SHERRI. What did you do?

CHARLIE. So, I kind of... uhm...

SHERRI. Charlie, spit it out.

CHARLIE. Ok, so I kind of pulled my applications?

SHERRI. What do you mean?

CHARLIE. I pulled them?

SHERRI. What does that mean, pulled them? What do you mean?

CHARLIE. I – I wrote to all the schools I applied to and asked them to stop considering my application.

SHERRI. What are you talking about?

CHARLIE. And then I wrote an editorial that's gonna be published today explaining what I did and why I did it.

SHERRI. You rescinded your applications?

CHARLIE. Yeah.

SHERRI. When did you do this?

CHARLIE. A week ago.

SHERRI. Are you being serious?

CHARLIE. Yeah.

SHERRI. You're serious?

CHARLIE. Yeah.

SHERRI. Close the door.

CHARLIE. What?

SHERRI. Close my office door.

(**CHARLIE** *closes the door.*)

What the fuck were you thinking?

CHARLIE. So you're not proud of me?

SHERRI. Proud of – are you out of your mind?

CHARLIE. I was trying to be – I was trying to live, to be the change I wanted to see in the world.

SHERRI. Fuck the change. You pulled your applications?

CHARLIE. If there are going to be new voices at the table, someone has to stand up and offer someone else his seat –

SHERRI. Are you OUT of your MIND?

CHARLIE. I'm still gonna go to college, just, community college.

SHERRI. Community College!

CHARLIE. You don't have to go to an Ivy to be successful. A lot of smart people didn't even go to college.

SHERRI. Charlie.

CHARLIE. Mark Zuckerberg didn't finish school –

SHERRI. He went to Harvard!

CHARLIE. Yeah but he dropped out.

SHERRI. Of *Harvard*!

CHARLIE. But –

SHERRI. Charlie! This is not a game! Why do you think Dad and I have been so hard on you the last four years? Because where you go to school MATTERS. It Matters. A kid who graduates from Brown and a kid who graduates from community college are going to have very different lives, as a general rule.

CHARLIE. But what about diversity?

SHERRI. We're not talking about diversity, we're talking about YOU Charlie, YOU.

CHARLIE. But don't I have a responsibility to do my part to make the world look the way I want it to look?

SHERRI. No.

CHARLIE. No?

SHERRI. No. Leave that to the admissions officers, ok? You're not going after the spots for minorities. You're going up for the white boy spots. So you take that white boy spot.

CHARLIE. But I don't want it. And I can do something about it, which is why...

SHERRI. Which is why, what?

CHARLIE. There's one more part. Of the editorial.

SHERRI. What is it?

CHARLIE. I probably should have run this by you before, I realize that now, but – hindsight's twenty-twenty, right?

SHERRI. What did you do? What *else* did you do?

CHARLIE. So, this is the question, right, that I've been asking myself. What can I do? I can recuse myself, but is that enough? Part of why colleges'll want me is I can pay my own way but, knowing my white parents are paying for their white son to go to school when a totally deserving student of color doesn't get to come to Hillcrest next fall because there isn't enough financial aid –

SHERRI. No.

CHARLIE. Doesn't that make you a little sick to your stomach?

SHERRI. No.

CHARLIE. I would like to donate the money you would have spent on my college to start a scholarship for a student of color at Hillcrest. So you can reach twenty percent. Now you have the money.

    (Beat.)

SHERRI. You wrote that? In the paper?

CHARLIE. Yes, my – my editorial says I will be, I am publicly asking my parents to donate my college tuition to endow a scholarship for a student of color at Hillcrest.

SHERRI. That is NOT your money to give away.

CHARLIE. It's not exactly yours, either, but...

SHERRI. ExCUSE me?

CHARLIE. I'm sorry, but that college fund is a big ole pile of white privilege.

SHERRI. No, Charlie, that money is money your dad and I worked very, very hard to save, and you didn't.

CHARLIE. You got to a place where you could even earn enough to save thousands of dollars every year because you've been advantaged your whole life.

SHERRI. I'm a middle-aged woman!

CHARLIE. If you'd had to pay reparations, you probably –

SHERRI. *Reparations* for *slavery* is not a personal decision teenage boys get to make with their parents' money.

CHARLIE. Mom! Why do the descendants of slave owners, and people who look like them, still have almost all the power and wealth in this country? How much has actually changed?

SHERRI. This can still be undone. Maybe this can –

CHARLIE. Mom.

SHERRI. I know Diane, at Dartmouth. And I know – I think Fred still runs Bowdoin's admissions.

CHARLIE. Mom.

SHERRI. Or maybe he took over Reed. I can – this can be undone.

CHARLIE. Mom. Mom.

I don't want you to use your pull to undo something.

SHERRI. You are crazy if you think I'm not about to call these schools and beg them to reconsider your application.

CHARLIE. I am asking you not to do that. Please Mom. Please.

(Beat.)

SHERRI. (Breathless.) Charlie.

CHARLIE. This is what I want.

SHERRI. This is what you want?

CHARLIE. This is what I want.

SHERRI. What do you even know about community college? You don't even know what you're talking about. Charlie. You're not going –

CHARLIE. There's nothing wrong with community college.

SHERRI. YOU are not going to COMMUNITY COLLEGE.

CHARLIE. Why? Because I'm privileged? And white, and male, and upper-middle-class?

SHERRI. Because you're smart, and gifted, at the top of your class at one of the country's finest schools, and your mind, and what you are capable of, is more than most. You're capable of more. And so you should have the best opportunities so that you can reach your full potential, because what you have to bring to the table, when you're not acting like a complete and total idiot, is more than most, sweetheart, and I don't even say that as your mother, but as an administrator at the school you attend. You're one of our very best, our finest. You want to change the world, then change it, but you don't change it by taking yourself out of the running.

CHARLIE. Anyone could be where I am if they'd had the advantages I've had. I'm not special.

SHERRI. How wrong you are.

CHARLIE. You can't pretend all of a sudden you're rooting for me.

SHERRI. What?

CHARLIE. You only like me cause I'm your kid. If I wasn't your kid, I'd be just another white guy, and you don't really have like a lot of fond feelings about white guys.

SHERRI. How can you say that?

CHARLIE. Because that's basically what you've been saying to me my whole life.

SHERRI. That's not true.

CHARLIE. Mom! WE BREAK OUT WINE, when four extra minorities apply to Hillcrest. We break out wine. When was the last time we broke out wine cause a really smart white guy decided to come to Hillcrest? And you didn't break out the fancy stuff when that paunchy middle-aged white poet came to stay with us last year. But the year before, when that other guy was here, what's his name –

SHERRI. *(Intense Spanish accent.)* Alejandro Ramirez.

CHARLIE. Right. There. Exactly.

SHERRI. Exactly what?

CHARLIE. Listen to how you say his name!

SHERRI. That's his name.

CHARLIE. Yeah but you like, relish saying it.

SHERRI. It's his name, Charlie!

CHARLIE. Say the name of the country he was from.

SHERRI. Why should I –

CHARLIE. What country was he from, just say it –

SHERRI. I'm not in the mood to play games –

CHARLIE. Just say it –

SHERRI. *(Same intense accent.)* NICARAGUA.

CHARLIE. Thank you. Exactly.

SHERRI. Exactly *what*?

CHARLIE. When the paunchy white dude from Connecticut stayed with us, you couldn't have cared less, but –

SHERRI. Because I didn't like him. I actually liked Alejandro! I'm allowed to like someone more than someone else.

CHARLIE. You decided to like him. You liked Alejandro before he ever came here. And you knew you didn't like middle-aged paunchy before he ever came here, too.

SHERRI. I... I happen to *love* white men.

CHARLIE. Ha!

SHERRI. I married a white man. My son is a white man. Some of my best friends are white men.

CHARLIE. Mom. That's literally the first time I've ever heard you say something positive about white men in my entire life.

SHERRI. That's not true.

CHARLIE. I'm not criticizing you. But you can't pretend now like it doesn't make you feel better when you see anyone, ANYONE who ISN'T a white man getting ahead, because you're just happier. You are. It matters to you, somehow. And you know what? It matters to me too. Because it means, something's working. The same people aren't just being spit out into the same slots. That's what's about to happen to me. But I can do something about it.

SHERRI. By going to Community College?

CHARLIE. By not taking advantage of privileges I was born with that I did nothing to deserve.

SHERRI. Sweetie. Yes. People use what they have to get ahead. That's, like, Darwinian. But it doesn't make them wrong.

CHARLIE. Maybe. But it doesn't make them right either.

Take the money. Start the scholarship. It's the right thing to do.

SHERRI. You don't get to tell me how to spend my money.

CHARLIE. That's true. But I choose not to have it spent on me. I do get to make that choice. What you do with it, is up to you.

Anyway. I need to go to calc...

SHERRI. The second you walk out that door, I'm picking up the phone and calling every school back –

CHARLIE. If you did that, you would be seriously betraying my trust. And my wishes. I know you look at me and you just see a kid, a stupid kid who doesn't get it. But maybe I get it more than anyone. At least do me the courtesy of assuming I have a brain, a good, high-functioning, intelligent brain, and that I thought through my actions, I considered the consequences, and I made a decision. Maybe it's not the decision you would have made for me but it's my decision. And I really hope you can honor it.

(He's about to exit, then stops.)

Mom?

SHERRI. Yes?

CHARLIE. What's for dinner tonight?

SHERRI. I... I got some salmon, I was gonna make.

CHARLIE. Oh. Ok.

(He exits. Beat.)

(Later that day.)

(Sherri's office. **BILL** *paces.)*

BILL. Sherri?

SHERRI. I know.

BILL. I hate him.

SHERRI. I – wait, what?

BILL. I hate him. I don't care. I *hate* him.

SHERRI. Ok that is not the appropriate – that is not the reaction I thought you were going to –

BILL. He did this to humiliate us.

SHERRI. No that, that is not why he –

BILL. Do you know how people were looking at me just now? I, I can't even go outside. A *tenth*-grader just shook my hand to thank me for starting the scholarship. I hate him.

SHERRI. Please stop saying you hate our son.

BILL. Is he insane? I think he might be clinically insane. This is when it happens, when boys lose their minds. One minute they're normal the next they're on a plane to the Middle East, joining ISIS. It happens that fast.

SHERRI. He's not joining ISIS. He's eighteen and confused. He has no idea what he wants.

BILL. And he'll figure that out right quick at community college. He wants to throw his life away? Be my guest. Guess who's done caring? This guy. I got him to eighteen, he's on his own. Sayonara, Charlie.

SHERRI. You know what, Bill? This isn't your decision to make. It's mine.

BILL. Oh is it?

SHERRI. Yes.

BILL. And why's that?

SHERRI. Because I'm his mother. I'm his mother. I made him, I fed –

BILL. Pretty sure I had something to do with making him –

SHERRI. I am not letting *my son* throw his life away.

BILL. You can't keep – maybe part of why he acts so erratically is because he knows you'll be there to helicopter in and clean up his messes. But there comes a point when, he has to learn from his own mistakes?

SHERRI. That may be, but, not today.

BILL. Well I disagree.

SHERRI. Overruled.

BILL. Excuse me?

SHERRI. Over fucking ruled.

> *(Beat.)*

This is what's gonna happen: *We* are going to talk to Sondra. *We* are going to call every one of these schools, starting with Yale, and see what can be undone, who we know, what we can do to get him reconsidered, even at one of his safeties, ok, even at *Bucknell*. And whatever your personal views, you are going to *swallow your pride* and just fucking be with me on this one. Ok? Just be with me.

> *(Beat.)*

BILL. Maybe you should talk to Ginnie.

SHERRI. Why?

BILL. Isn't her brother's wife a dean at Middlebury, or something?

> *(**SHERRI** thinks.)*
>
> *(She has to do this.)*
>
> *(Fuck.)*

(Later.)

(Sherri's office. **GINNIE** *stands in her coat. A beat.)*

GINNIE. No.

SHERRI. Really?

GINNIE. Really.

SHERRI. Ginnie, I know you were upset about the things you felt Charlie said to you, but –

GINNIE. I'm not upset at Charlie, this has nothing to do with him.

SHERRI. I know you were upset with me, and I apologize to you, and I did apologize to you, and I reached out to you...

GINNIE. You cannot unsay the things you said.

SHERRI. But I don't think I ever said –

GINNIE. Sherri. You made it very clear what your feelings were that day. Crystal clear. You took fifteen years of friendship and went:

> *(She brushes her hands together.)*

I made it very clear in my last email, I want nothing to do with you.

SHERRI. Ginnie. I apologized.

GINNIE. You don't get it. You think it's... you think it's this little thing. You know? *He got in cause he's Black.* You are not the mother of a Black child, so you might not be able to understand this, but that line of thinking follows my son everywhere. Everywhere. And it's amplified. That's just the subtle version of it. And when it's amplified, it's scary as hell. I've tried to shield him the best I know how, but I never thought I'd have to shield him from the woman who's practically been his godmother. I didn't see that coming. And you know what?

> *(She has more to say, but stops herself.)*

Don't ask me for help again. I have no help I want to offer you.

SHERRI. We spent all afternoon calling schools. It's too late. One person thought Charlie could maybe get on a waitlist but she wasn't sure. All I am asking is if you could call your sister-in-law. Forget me. Don't even think about me. But, Charlie. I know this isn't what you want for him.

GINNIE. I want for Charlie whatever Charlie wants for Charlie.

SHERRI. No, no. Our brightest kids should not take themselves out of the running, that's not how we change things.

GINNIE. Polar ice caps melt faster than what you've managed to change here.

SHERRI. How can you say that? People's lives have – Marshall Washington clerked at the *Supreme* Court –

GINNIE. Marshall Washington was going to be something whether he came to Hillcrest or not.

SHERRI. No I – I know that…

GINNIE. Do you? Because you bring him up all the time, your great success story but, Marshall was miserable here.

SHERRI. He wasn't mis–

GINNIE. Sherri! You don't know the first thing about it! Marshall used to go talk to Don, after class – we even had him over to the house a few times, just so he had a place to let it out. You have no idea. The faculty, the administration, the whole school acted like they *made* him. Or else, they treated him like this miraculous anomaly – a really smart Black kid at Hillcrest. As if there aren't literally millions of perfectly smart Black kids running around all over the country. As if the issue is with them. As if it's their fault no one ever sees them.

SHERRI. All I *do* is look for those kids, fight so this place looks different.

GINNIE. You want things to look different, but I'm not sure you want them to *be* different. Cause if they were, you wouldn't be at the center of it all, and I think that would scare you. You want faces for your brochure and numbers you can use in your statistics, but when you can't use them... you don't see those kids at all. It's like they've been... invisible to you.

(*Beat.*)

SHERRI. You think, you think *Perry* has been invisible to me? You think I don't see your son, love your son. You know I do.

(**GINNIE** *does know this.*)

And I know, you love Charlie.

I am begging you.

(**GINNIE** *is about to say no.*)

If you're gonna say no, just please don't say it out loud.

GINNIE. I'm gonna say no.

SHERRI. Ginnie?

GINNIE. I'm going to be late for Perry's game. Take care.

(*She leaves.*)

(**BILL** *and* **SHERRI** *sit in the living room. Both on their computers, working.*)

(*Very quietly,* **CHARLIE** *enters the room. He looks at his parents. He is very still. He stares at them for a long time. They don't notice.*)

(*There is something slightly ominous in his demeanor. Finally:*)

CHARLIE. Who did this?

SHERRI. Jesus you scared me.

CHARLIE. Who did this?

BILL. Did what?

SHERRI. How long have you been standing there?

CHARLIE. I just got into Middlebury.

SHERRI. Oh my god!! Oh my god oh my god oh shit oh my –

(*She jumps in the air. She goes to hug* **CHARLIE.** *He doesn't want a hug.*)

CHARLIE. Who did this?

(*To* **SHERRI.**) It was you. Wasn't it?

SHERRI. You got into Middlebury!

CHARLIE. Who did this?

BILL. We both did.

SHERRI. Oh my god!

CHARLIE. Why would you do this to me? When I explicitly asked you –

SHERRI. You got into Middlebury!

CHARLIE. I'm not going.

SHERRI. Oh yes you are.

CHARLIE. Oh no I'm not.

SHERRI. Oh Yes. You. Are.

CHARLIE. No. I'm going to –

SHERRI. To community college? Guess what? That's not happening.

BILL. Not happening.

SHERRI. Not happening.

CHARLIE. Oh, it's happening.

SHERRI. No, it's not.

BILL. You want to go to community college, you're paying for it.

SHERRI. Bill.

CHARLIE. I know! That was the whole point!

BILL. Terrific. Great.

SHERRI. Bill.

BILL. Enjoy paying for that.

SHERRI. Bill.

BILL. I can tell you from firsthand experience it's a great joy to earn the kind of money you need to pay for college. And you're paying all your expenses, cause you're not living under my roof while you go to community college.

CHARLIE. I'm eighteen, I can do what I want.

BILL. Great. You do that Charlie.

SHERRI. No, you won't do that. Bill. *(Unspoken: Be with me.)*

Charlie, do you understand the difference between going to Middlebury and going to community college?

CHARLIE. That's not the point. That is not why I'm doing this.

BILL. We know, we know, you're doing it cause you're a martyr. The great white martyr. But let's think this through a second. See, you're not living *here* while you go to some shit school, so, what are you gonna do? You'll need someplace to live. Maybe you'll find a nice little moldy basement apartment somewhere, and then you'll get a job, tossing pizzas, or bussing tables to pay for said shithole apartment. You'll never see your friends, you'll never do anything fun because you'll be scrimping and saving to pay for tuition and cell phone bills and electric bills and health insurance so you can make some point about white privilege by taking shitty classes at some podunk piece of shit little school? I don't think so. No. What you're gonna do is, you're gonna go to Middlebury, which we will pay for, and you're gonna get your little degree in English or History or whatever subject strikes your little fancy and then you can go off and do whatever you want. But I've got a feeling, and – Sherri, cover your ears – I've got a feeling you're gonna be up in Vermont this winter, sleeping with some very attractive young undergraduate because you're gonna have time to do things like that because you're not gonna have to worry about running from the pizza shift to the busboy shift, and right as you're all warm and toasty in your little dorm room, pumping away at this hot little undergrad you're gonna think: thanks Dad.

SHERRI. Bill!

BILL. Dad was right. This really is a whole lot better than Community College.

(*To* **SHERRI**.) How's *that* for fucking being with you?

(*Beat.*)

SHERRI. You're gonna love Middlebury, I know it.

CHARLIE. Mom. No.

SHERRI. Come here, honey.

CHARLIE. You guys make no sense. Everything I do is wrong. It's really confusing.

BILL. It's not confusing. It's very simple. We love you, we want the best for you.

CHARLIE. No, you want me to be just like you, cause I guess you think you're like, nailing life, but actually, my worst nightmare would be turning out like you.

You can't even see yourself, can you? You can't even *see* yourself.

You think you spent your life championing the underdog; did you ever stop to think about who got shoved out of the way so you could do it? You're happy to make the world a better place, as long as it doesn't cost you anything. That's what your tombstone should say: Bill Mason made the world a better place, and it didn't cost him a thing. Well that's not fair, it did cost you one thing: occasionally, you let yourself feel guilty, but that's like, the only price you're willing to pay to still get EVERYTHING YOU WANT. Call me naive, but if people could make the world fairer without sacrificing *anything*, it would have happened by now. It hasn't. You're like the last generation of white men who could say one thing, do another, and just keep climbing the stairs of your ivory tower. I'm trying to be intentional about my climb. How can I honestly look at any situation, any school I want to go to, any job I might want, and think, that place should really be more diverse, but also, may I have a seat at this table? If you give me a seat, I swear I'll do everything I can to keep out all the other people who look like me. What is honorable about that? I don't want to blindly climb my way to the top, pretend everything's gonna take care of itself while I get as far as I possibly can, and then *burn* the staircase behind me and try to make a difference over there, down there, in some area that doesn't affect me at all. The way you did. The way you fucking did. You think you're like some kind of hero? Look in a mirror Dad: you're not a hero. You're a hypocrite.

SHERRI. ENOUGH! Enough. This stops now. The debate is over. Bill. Charlie. You go to Middlebury. The end.

CHARLIE. But that's not what I want.

SHERRI. You don't have a choice.

CHARLIE. How do I not have a choice? IT'S MY LIFE! Legally, I can –

SHERRI. FUCK LEGALLY CHARLIE! JUST STOP IT! STOP IT! STOP!!!!

Just go to Middlebury, ok? Ple–

CHARLIE. But then you won't have money for the scholarship.

SHERRI. Oh well.

CHARLIE. But how is that fair?

SHERRI. Because it is.

CHARLIE. How is that fair?

SHERRI. Because I said so.

CHARLIE. But how is it –

SHERRI. Because you're my son! You are my son.

> *(Beat.)*

Go to Middlebury, ok? Accept their offer and go. You don't have to understand why. Just go.

> *(Beat.)*

> *(**CHARLIE** looks younger than he ever has. He walks up the stairs, very slowly, and closes his bedroom door.)*

> *(**SHERRI** stands at the bottom of the stairs and looks up.)*

> *(**BILL** almost speaks to her, then chooses not to.)*

> *(After a beat, he opens his computer and turns on a baseball game.)*

> *(We hear the sounds of it, the announcers talking, the fans.* He's not cheering or very engaged, but he watches.)*

> *(**SHERRI** is now more alone than ever.)*

> *(Then **BILL** exits. **SHERRI** has nowhere to go. She stands by the staircase, where she knows, in a room just above her, her little boy is also sitting by himself, alone. Before she lets herself feel too much, she turns away.)*

---

*A license to produce *Admissions* does not include a performance license for any third-party or copyrighted recordings. Licensees should create their own.

(Sherri's office.)

ROBERTA. Sherri?

SHERRI. Come in.

ROBERTA. I just heard, Charlie's going to Middlebury? That's wonderful! Congratulations.

SHERRI. Thank you.

ROBERTA. My nephew did a summer program there, learned Mandarin Chinese in six weeks! It was wild! It's a wonderful school.

SHERRI. It is.

ROBERTA. And then you and Bill will have an empty nest. It's a big adjustment.

SHERRI. Eighteen years really, flew by.

ROBERTA. They go faster from here, I can tell you that.

SHERRI. Oh, terrific.

ROBERTA. Yeah. But you have time. There's still the summer, graduation, prom. Does Charlie have a prom date yet?

SHERRI. He does.

ROBERTA. May I ask, whom?

(Quick beat.)

SHERRI. Olive Opatovsky.

ROBERTA. Isn't that nice. Just friends, or...

SHERRI. Just friends, I think.

ROBERTA. Isn't that nice.

Well. I was only stopping by because...

(She holds up the admissions catalogue.)

Hot off the presses. I think it turned out well.

SHERRI. Oh good. Good.

ROBERTA. There are nineteen pictures with students of color. All... *obvious.*

SHERRI. Ok.

ROBERTA. And I realized: nineteen photos, and now we're nineteen percent minority next fall, it's a sign. If you believe in those kind of things. Which I do, but...

SHERRI. Ok.

ROBERTA. And... I included the photo of Perry and Charlie playing basketball. I didn't count it in the statistics, but I figured, it's probably the last catalogue Charlie'll be in. And it's such a sweet picture.

> (*She opens the catalogue to the published photo and puts it on Sherri's desk.* **SHERRI** *looks at it.*)

SHERRI. Oh. That's really nice. That's... really... Thanks.

ROBERTA. And there's four photos of faculty of color. So, I hope you're pleased.

> (**SHERRI** *stares at the photo of her son. Then she looks up.*)

SHERRI. It's perfect.

> (*Blackout.*)

End of Play